The Foggy, Foggy Forest

CANDLEWICK PRESS
CAMBRIDGE, MASSACHUSETTS

Nick Sharratt

What can this be in the foggy, foggy forest?

A little elf all by himself.

What can this be in the foggy, foggy forest?

Three brown bears in picnic chairs.

What can this be in the foggy, foggy forest?

A fairy queen on a trampoline.

What can this be in the foggy, foggy forest?

A unicorn playing a horn.

What can this be in the foggy, foggy forest?

Goldilocks with a candy box.

What can this be in the foggy, foggy forest?

A witch on a broom . . .

with a motor—*vroom, vroom!*

What can this be in the foggy, foggy forest?

An ogre doing yoga.

What can this be in the foggy, foggy forest?

in a water-pistol fight.

What can this be in the foggy, foggy forest?

selling ice cream—oh, what luck!

And what can *that* be over there?

Hooray! Hooray! A traveling fair!